APRIL'S KITTENS

APRIL'S

STORY AND PICTURES BY

HARPER & BROTHERS PUBLISHERS

KITTENS

CLARE TURLAY NEWBERRY

NEW YORK AND LONDON 1940

Hand-set in Bulmer type at the Golden Hind Press, Madison, N. J.

To

Fletcher H. Burdett

THERE WAS ONCE a nice little girl named April, who lived in New York City with her mother, her father, and a black cat called Sheba.

Nobody has much room in New York because so many people are trying to live there at the same time. So April and her mother and father and Sheba lived all crowded up together in a very small apartment. It was so small that there wasn't even room in it for April to have a real bed, and although she was six she still slept in a crib.

April's father called it a "one-cat" apartment, and he often warned Sheba against having a family.

"One cat is all very well," he would say, smoothing her sleek black head, "but one is quite enough. Remember that, Sheba! This is a strictly one-cat apartment."

Sheba, however, paid not the slightest attention. She went right ahead and had kittens, three of them, one black and two with tiger-stripes. Of course April was enchanted. All day long she sat on the floor beside Sheba's box and adored them. It was all her mother could do to pry her away from them long enough to brush her hair or wash her face or eat her meals. All she wanted to do was sit on the floor and watch Sheba's kittens.

Her father was not nearly so pleased with them.

"Four cats in an apartment this size is exactly three too many," he grumbled. "You will have to do something about those kittens, Margaret. And the sooner the better, before April gets attached to them."

"Now, Charles, those kittens can't possibly bother you while they're so tiny. They don't make any noise, and they're too little to climb out of the box. Don't worry, we'll find homes for them all in good time."

April did not listen. She was much too busy watching the kittens. One of the striped ones had a white nose and forehead, which made her look as though her hair were parted in the middle. Her little paws were white, too, and the tiny pads on

· 8 ·

them were of the tenderest pink. April ran a gentle forefinger over her little furry head and gave a sigh of pure happiness. Then she stroked the other two and Sheba, so they wouldn't feel neglected.

It was plain to her that Daddy was mistaken about there being room in the apartment for only one cat. Here they were with four, and how much more delightful life was for everyone! So April thought.

"What *are* we going to name them, Mummy?" she asked one day.

"Well, let's see now," said her mother, glancing up from the dress she was lengthening for April, "how about 'Tommy'? Or 'Tiger'? Or 'Tabby'?"

April considered, frowning seriously. Then she shook her head.

"No, Mummy, I don't like any of those."

"Well, then, how about 'Midge'? Or 'Mouser'? Or how about 'Midnight' for the little black one?"

"No-o, Mummy, I don't like any of those, either," said April to each suggestion, and she begged her mother to think of some more names. This went on for days. At last her father took a hand.

"I'm going to name those kittens myself, here and now, and get it settled," he announced one morning, and he strode across the room to the kitten box. The kittens already had their eyes open and were busily crawling over, under, and around Sheba and each other. It was certainly high time they had names.

"H'm," said April's father, regarding them thoughtfully. He

tickled the black one's fat little tummy and they all laughed to see it stretch and yawn, showing a pink-lined mouth and the tiniest white teeth in the world.

"Kitten, I name you—*Charcoal*," he said impressively, and April giggled her approval.

He touched the next kitten, the tiger-striped one without any white on it.

"Kitten, I name you—*Butch!*"

"Daddy, you're good!" laughed April. "He looks as if his name was Butch."

"His name *is* Butch," said her father firmly. And then he touched the third and last kitten, the sweet white-faced one, with her hair parted in the middle. April caught her breath.

"Oh, Daddy, do be careful of that one."

"Here goes," said her father. "Kitten, I name you—*Brenda*. There you are, April—Charcoal, Butch, and Brenda."

"Brenda," repeated April, trying it out. "Daddy, you're good. You're a wonderful kitten-namer!"

"Thank you, April. I don't think I'm so bad myself," said her father. He turned to her mother.

"Now that they're all properly named, what are we going to do with them, Margaret? In a few more days they'll be climbing out of the box and then this place will be simply swarming with kittens. You won't be able to walk across the room without stepping on them. Have you found anyone to take them yet?"

His words brought forth a wail of protest from April.

Butch

"Oh, *Daddy*! Aren't we going to *keep* them?"

"Charles, dear," murmured her mother, "that wasn't tactful."

"I know, I know," he said hastily, with an uneasy glance at April's face. "Well, Margaret, I told you in the beginning you'd better do something before she got attached to them. Now what are we going to do?"

"Let's keep them, Mummy, *please* let's keep them!" begged April.

Her mother thought for a moment.

"Why don't we let April keep one of the kittens, and give away Sheba and the other two?" she suggested. April's father brightened.

"The very thing!" he agreed heartily. "Why didn't we think of that before? You'd rather have a kitten to play with, wouldn't you, honey?"

"Of course she would," said her mother soothingly. "And we'll find nice homes for the others. How would that be, darling?"

April looked down at the kittens, batting her eyelashes rapidly to keep back the tears. If she had to choose one of them there was no doubt which it would be. She loved them all, but Brenda, dear little Brenda, with the tiny white feet and her hair parted sweetly in the middle, was far and away her favorite. But how could she give up Sheba?

"Do we really have to give Sheba away if we keep a kitten?" she faltered.

Brenda

"I'm afraid so, dear. You know it bothers Daddy to have too many cats around."

April sighed heavily and smoothed Sheba's black velvet fur. Sheba, who was scrubbing little Charcoal, gave her hand a sudden lick with her rough tongue. And at that April's tears spilled over and dripped slowly onto the kittens, making wet patches in their soft fur.

"But what shall we do with Sheba, Mummy?"

"Oh, I don't know," said her mother cheerfully. "Perhaps Aunt Helen would take her. Sheba would like to live in the country, I'm sure. But if you'd rather keep her and give away the kittens, it's all right. Just so long as we don't have more than one cat. That's what Daddy said, you know."

"Yes, Mummy, I know," said April huskily.

The next day was a most important one. The kittens had their first dish of milk. They didn't know what it was, to begin with, but when their noses had been pushed into it several times they began to get the idea. Then they tried to lap, but they had a hard time of it. Either their little bobbing heads didn't quite reach the milk, or else they dipped into it too far and got it up their noses, which made them sneeze and shake their heads. The silly little things didn't know enough even to keep their feet out of the dish, and they had to be lifted out of it again and again.

"Never mind, kittens, you'll learn," said April's mother. She put them back in the box and Sheba gave them each a good

Pretty soon they could lap milk
almost as well as grown-up cats.

bath. They needed it, too, for their faces were all milky and their paws were sopping.

Every day after that they had some milk in a dish. And every day they sneezed and bobbled less, and got more of the milk down their throats and less on their paws and whiskers. Pretty soon they could lap it almost as well as grown-up cats.

One afternoon Mrs. Dalton, who was a friend of April's mother, came to tea. She brought her little boy with her.

"This is Geoffrey, April," said April's mother.

The two children shook hands timidly and then backed off and stared bashfully at each other. Geoffrey tugged at his mother's sleeve.

"Mummy, Mummy!" he whispered urgently, "where are the kitties? You said there would be kitties!"

"Geoffrey is going to take one of Sheba's kittens home with him, April," said her mother, "and then, whenever we go to Geoffrey's house you can play with the kitten again. Won't that be nice?"

"Yes, Mummy," answered April in a low voice. She was very shy with strangers.

They all went into the living-room to look at the kittens.

"*Kitties!*" cried Geoffrey rapturously, and he plumped down on his knees beside the box.

"Oh, Geoffrey, aren't they adorable!" exclaimed his mother. "Which one do you want, darling? Does it matter which one he picks?"

· 18 ·

Butch and Brenda

"Why, no, of course not," said April's mother politely.

April's heart sank. She had never said she loved Brenda the best—she hadn't wanted to hurt the other kittens' feelings. And now she was too shy to say anything, with Mrs. Dalton and Geoffrey there. She stood close to her mother and waited unhappily while they fondled first one squirming kitten and then another.

"April is crazy about all of them," said her mother. "She thinks we ought to keep all three of them and the mother cat as well." And she and Mrs. Dalton laughed as though she had said something very funny.

At last Geoffrey held up little Butch.

"I want this kitty," he announced, to April's relief. "I like him the best."

While they had tea April's mother explained to Mrs. Dalton how to take care of Butch and feed him properly. And Mrs. Dalton promised to do everything just right, and to see that Geoffrey didn't play too hard with him, for Geoffrey was only four and might not know at first just how to treat a kitten.

After tea the visitors went home, with Butch tucked snugly under Geoffrey's windbreaker.

The next day Miss Elwell came to April's house. Miss Elwell was extremely fond of cats and had two enormous ones of her own, although she lived in a small apartment. However, having no husband or children, she naturally had more room for cats.

"Wouldn't you like to adopt one of our kittens, Miss Elwell?"

asked April's mother.

"Heavens, no!" cried Miss Elwell, "I already have too many cats. You should see my meat bill—it's simply appalling!"

But when she saw Charcoal and Brenda playing hide-and-seek among the sofa pillows she began to weaken.

"Oh, the sweet things! The little darlings!" she kept saying over and over. And presently she had decided to take one after all.

"May I have either one?" she asked, reaching for Brenda.

"Of course, Miss Elwell, either one you like," said April's mother, and April watched anxiously while Miss Elwell petted first Brenda, then Charcoal, then Brenda again. Finally she picked up Charcoal and held him against her cheek.

"I believe I'll take this one, if I may," she said. "My other cats are both black, so I may as well have a kitten that matches."

And April smiled happily, for she still had Brenda.

"I hope your grown cats won't frighten Charcoal," said April's mother. "They're so big and he's so little."

Miss Elwell laughed.

"It will be just the other way around," she said. "The big cats will be afraid of Charcoal at first. But after a day or two they'll be very happy together."

So Miss Elwell took Charcoal home with her, and there was only Sheba and Brenda left.

"Tomorrow is Sunday so we may as well take Sheba out to Aunt Helen's," said April's mother. "Daddy can drive us out." Catching sight of April's woebegone face she added reproach-

Charcoal

At first the big cats were

afraid of little Charcoal!

fully, "You aren't going to be naughty about it, are you, darling? You know what Daddy said."

April swallowed hard and was silent. She was trying to be good, but it was hard work. That evening she scarcely noticed the kitten. Instead, she followed Sheba about, showering her with attentions. She fed Sheba her ground meat by hand, for Sheba's greater enjoyment, and every time she lay down for a catnap April at once covered her tenderly with a doll's blanket.

That night April did not fall asleep as usual. She lay wide awake in her crib, thinking about poor Sheba. Would Sheba be happy at Aunt Helen's house, she wondered. Or would she be lonely and miserable? Pretty soon voices floated in from the living-room.

"What will Helen say when we drive up tomorrow with a yowling cat in the back seat?" her father asked. "Does Helen want the cat?"

Her mother laughed a little.

"Well, not particularly, I'm afraid. She'd much rather have a kitten, of course. But she promised to take Sheba if no one else would. I suppose Helen can give her to one of the neighbors if *she* doesn't want to keep her."

There was a silence. Then April's father said:

"Poor old Sheba. I hope she does find a good home. She's such a nice cat."

"She *is* a nice cat," agreed her mother soberly. "I'd feel happier if we were keeping her and giving away the kitten.

· 26 ·

Most people like kittens— they're so cunning—but not many care anything about a grown cat they haven't raised themselves."

April's throat tightened painfully. She saw a vision that wrung her heart. Poor Sheba, taken squalling, frightened, and betrayed, to be turned loose in a strange place where no one cared for her. April pictured Sheba's grief and despair when she realized that her own family didn't want her. Most dreadful of all—Sheba would think that April no longer loved her. This was utterly unbearable, and suddenly April knew what she must do. There was no help for it—Brenda must go to Aunt Helen's instead. Aunt Helen wanted Brenda and would keep her and be kind to her.

At this moment April's mother stepped quietly into the bedroom. She leaned over April and laid a cool hand on her hot forehead.

"What's the matter, darling? Why aren't you asleep?"

"I'm all right, Mummy," said April miserably, "I just can't get comfortable." Then she flung her arms about her mother's neck.

"Oh, Mummy!" she wailed, "Aunt Helen can have Brenda! I want *Sheeeeeba!*" And she began to sob wildly.

"All right, darling, of course you shall keep Sheba, if you'd rather," soothed her mother. She led April out to the bathroom and washed her face and gave her a long drink of cold water to help her stop crying. The sobs died down into an occasional hiccup and soon April was back in bed again, with a clean hanky in her hand while her mother straightened up the tumbled bedding.

When she had finished tucking April in she went to the door and called April's father.

"Charles, come here a minute. I want to show you something."

April's father put down his newspaper and came in.

"What's the matter?" he asked.

"Look, Charles, April will have to have a new bed. She has outgrown this one."

He looked and it was perfectly true. April was very small for her age, and that was why she had slept in a crib so long. But now at last she had outgrown it. When she stretched out her toes touched the foot.

"You're right. She certainly can't sleep in that crib much longer. She'll have to have a real bed."

"But we can't get it into this apartment," her mother pointed out, "there just isn't room."

"Then we shall simply have to move into a larger apartment," said her father. "We need more room anyhow. We're much too crowded here."

April sat up.

"Daddy!" she cried, "when we get a new apartment, what kind will it be? I mean, will it be just another one-cat apartment like this one, or—or—" her voice broke and she gazed up at him imploringly. He hesitated for a moment. Then he said:

"Well, Margaret, what do you think? Shall we get a *two*-cat apartment this time?"

"Charles," replied her mother, "I think that's a splendid idea. What this family really needs is a good, roomy, two-cat apartment. What do you think, April?"

"Mummy," said April earnestly, "I think it would be just perfect!"

"Then it's settled," said her father with a smile. "We'll keep the two cats, and tomorrow morning we'll go apartment hunting."

April paused just long enough to give each of her parents a smothering hug. Then she ran out into the living-room to tell Sheba and Brenda the good news.

And when she was tucked into bed again, she made up a poem, because she was so happy. It was a Song for Cats, and this is how it went:

> I purr . . . and I purr . . .
> And I purr . . . and I purr . . .
> And I curl . . . up . . . warm.

Then April herself curled up warm and went to sleep.

The End